Dear Miss Perfect

A **Beast's** Guide to Proper Behavior

To Zoie,
May all your good times be beastly!
Sandra Dutton

by Sandra Dutton

Houghton Mifflin Company

Boston 2007

For Max, Kim, Ava,
Morganna, and Lila
—S.D.

Copyright © 2007 by Sandra Dutton

All rights reserved. For information about permission to reproduce selections from this book, write to
Permissions, Houghton Mifflin Company, 215 Park Avenue South, New York, New York 10003.

www.houghtonmifflinbooks.com

The text of this book is set in Diotima. • The illustrations are pen, ink, and watercolor.

Library of Congress Cataloging-in-Publication Data
Dutton, Sandra.
Dear Miss Perfect : a beast's guide to proper behavior / written and illustrated by Sandra Dutton.
p. cm.
Summary: An etiquette expert answers animal readers' questions about common concerns such as
getting along with parents, giving an oral report, and the importance of writing thank-you notes,
as well as more unusual ones, including how to avoid being eaten by one's parents.
ISBN-13: 978-0-618-67717-7 (hardcover) • ISBN-10: 0-618-67717-8 (hardcover)
[1. Etiquette—Fiction. 2. Advice columns—Fiction. 3. Animals—Fiction. 4. Humorous stories.] I. Title.
PZ7.D952Dea 2007
[E]—dc22   2006009815

Printed in Singapore • TWP 10 9 8 7 6 5 4 3 2 1

Do you keep your tail under your chair
to keep others from tripping?

Do you bring a note from home
if you have been hibernating?

Do you avoid pushing, snorting,
growling, stomping, hissing, stampeding,
and head butting?

Miss Perfect hopes so.

But why can't I be myself? you say.
I'm a Beast!

Be yourself! But never bite another
unless *you* would like to be bitten.

That's Miss Perfect's Golden Rule.

To Learn Best

Dear Miss Perfect,

I am in the fourth grade at
Chesterton Elementary School.
I sit in the second seat of the third row.

My problem is that I like to hang upside down.
Mama lets me do it at home. That's how I'm
most comfortable, and the way I learn best.

I have asked my teacher if I can't climb up
to one of the hanging lights, wrap my tail
around it, and study upside down.

She says **no.**

I think she's being mean.

> Your friend,
> Emily Possum

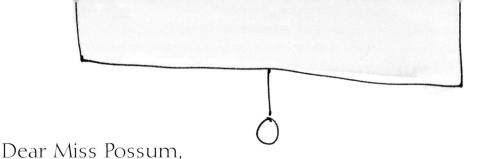

Dear Miss Possum,

Miss Perfect would like to suggest that perhaps
your teacher has a good reason for not allowing
you up there. Perhaps she is concerned that you
might hurt yourself or others should you fall.

Perhaps she is also concerned that during tests
you might not keep your eyes on your own paper.

Or that you might fall asleep.

However, Miss Perfect suspects that you do
learn best upside down.

Miss Possum, have you considered getting
a doctor's permission? He can assure your teacher
that you reach your maximum potential
only if you are allowed to hang upside down.

And you, Miss Possum, can assure her that you will
keep your eyes on your own paper during tests.

Onward and upward,

Miss Perfect

Seeking Agreement

Dear Miss Perfect,

I like my hair long and straight.
Mother says it's too straggly, so she made
me go to the beauty parlor for a permanent.

I look awful now. My hair is all frizzy and I
do not want to go to school.

I feel so bad, Miss Perfect, I would like to cut
my head off.

What can I do?

      Feeling ugly,
      Mary Ellen Yak

Dear Miss Yak,

First of all, Miss Perfect does not believe you should
cut off your head, no matter how ugly
you think you may look.

It is far more prudent to keep one's head and
work out a plan with your mother.

Certainly there is a hairstyle that you both can agree on.

Braids are nice. French knots are attractive.
Or, how about a trim and a gentle wave?

In the meantime, find a smart cap and sweater set
that can camouflage your curls until they grow out.

Have patience,

Miss Perfect

In Step

Dear Miss Perfect,

Yesterday afternoon I went to our school "Hot 100" Dance in the multipurpose room. I asked lots of girls to dance, but no one would be my partner.

Miss Perfect, I know all the dances.
I can rumba. I can samba. I can cha-cha-cha.
What should I do?

    Tired of dancing alone,
    Jonathan Porcupine

P.S. I keep my quills flat at all times.

Dear Mr. Porcupine,

You need a partner with thick skin.

I recommend a Rhinoceros. Even though they are
large, they are light on their feet. What a handsome
pair you would make, Mr. Porcupine!

And if you can't find a Rhinoceros, what about
a Hippo, an Elephant, or a Crocodile? Miss Perfect
believes you've simply been asking the wrong girls.

Search among the wallflowers,

Miss Perfect

Speaking Out

Dear Miss Perfect,

Next week we have to give
an oral book report.

Do you think it would be all right
if I memorized mine and
talked with my head in my shell?

Standing up in front of class
makes me nervous.

    Hoping to be sick,
    Rodney Turtle

P.S. I could glue knobs on my chest
and pretend I'm a radio.

Dear Mr. Turtle,

Pretending to be a radio is clever.
You might even wear an antenna.
But to hold the attention of your classmates
you'll need to keep your head out.

Why not pretend to be a news reporter?
Report the news of your book.

Miss Perfect believes you'll be so excited
about sharing, you'll forget to be nervous.

Heads up,

Miss Perfect

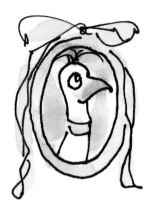

A Word from Miss Perfect on Food

Do you chew quietly at the table,
even when eating a large hunk of meat?

Do you brush the crumbs off your whiskers?

Are you open to trying new foods,
such as dandelions, or termite pizza?

No matter what you eat, Miss Perfect
believes you should do it politely,
with consideration for others.

Do not spit your seeds across the room.
Keep your elbows out of your soup.

And while you are at the table, remember
that slurping, smacking, belching, and
loud crunching are never proper,
even at a picnic.

Dining Out

Dear Miss Perfect,

I enjoy picking through the trash. It's my hobby.
Yesterday I found a meatball hero,
a half gallon of orange juice, a carton of eggs,
and a big round of liverwurst.

I took it home to my brothers and sisters.

Until now, I have been simply helping myself.
But I am wondering, Miss Perfect, would it be more
appropriate for me to ring the doorbell and ask
permission?

    Always on the lookout,
    Albert Raccoon

Dear Mr. Raccoon,

When Miss Perfect puts something in the
trash, she does not expect to retrieve it.
You do not, therefore, need
to ring the doorbell and ask permission.

I recommend, however, that you choose
only the most nutritious of snacks.
(You seem to be doing a good job.)

Inspect the cans quickly and quietly.
Be sure to clean up,
and put the lids on securely.

Tidiness counts,

Miss Perfect

Needs Some Variety

Dear Miss Perfect,

My mother is an Anteater and I am adopted.
I love my mother very much. She reads me stories
and even bought me a trampoline for the backyard.

My problem is that all she serves for dinner is ants.
I'm tired of ants.

What can I do?

Searching for possibilities,
Ricky Platypus

Dear Mr. Platypus,

Though ants are not Miss Perfect's favorite food,
she must tell you that ants are an excellent source
of vitamins and protein. They are also recommended
for long hikes and feats of endurance. In fact, if you had
to get along with one food only, ants would be that food.

That said, Miss Perfect sympathizes.
She herself would not like a diet wholly made up of ants.

Miss Perfect recommends that you politely ask
your mother if she would mind sprinkling ants
over a baked potato. This way you are subtly introducing
her to new food.

You might also use your allowance to buy an especially
delicious vanilla ice cream, and serve your mother a dish.
Sprinkle it generously with the ants and see what she says.
I'll bet you'll win her over.

Venture with tact,

Miss Perfect

Dinner Etiquette

Dear Miss Perfect,

I have a rather long nose. In fact, it's
six feet long. It never gets in the way
at picnics and wienie roasts, but I am
wondering where to place it at the table.

I know that I may eat with my trunk,
but where do I put it between courses?

My dad says it's okay to rest it
on the table.

What do you say, Miss Perfect?

    Sincerely,

    Arthur B. Elephant

Dear Mr. Elephant,

I must tell you that trunks, like elbows,
do not belong on the table.

You are wise to learn the proper etiquette.

Between courses you should place your trunk
to your left if you are right-footed
or to your right if you are left-footed.

Should you wish to trumpet
your enjoyment at the end of a meal,
simply raise your trunk high above everyone's head
and give a hearty elephant bellow.

Bon appetit,

Miss Perfect

Mother's Day Feast

Dear Miss Perfect,

I am making a three-course breakfast for
my mother on Mother's Day.
I'm thinking of having slugs on toast,
fried worms, and a large cup of hot chocolate.

But I am wondering, Miss Perfect, which should
I serve first, the slugs or the worms?

Hoping to please,
Bartley Hedgehog

Dear Mr. Hedgehog,

Miss Perfect is delighted that you are planning
a treat for your mother on Mother's Day.

Slugs should always be served first.
They make a lovely appetizer, and you
might sprinkle on a little Tabasco for accent.

Fried worms should come second.
They're a hearty main dish.

Hot chocolate should come last, as dessert.

Have you picked Mother a bouquet of flowers?
Miss Perfect recommends violets in a pretty vase.

Blessings to you,

Miss Perfect

Being a Lady

Dear Miss Perfect,

Yesterday I was invited to a birthday party
at my friend Billy Hamster's. I was having a great time
until Mrs. Hamster served the cake. She gave each of
the guests a piece, and then put a whole wedge of
cake on a plate and handed it to me.

"I know you've got a **big** appetite!" she said.

I was so embarrassed.

Miss Perfect, I am a lady. When I am at a party,
I would like to receive the same sized portion as everyone else.

Whatever am I to do?

> Just hoping to fit in,
>
> Justina Pig

Dear Miss Pig,

My, my, Miss Perfect is usually having to help people who feel they have been slighted, but you are being treated almost as a guest of honor.

Why not dig in and enjoy! I'll bet Billy Hamster wishes he could eat as much as you.

So, Miss Pig, I think you can eat a full wedge of cake and still be a lady!

Dig in,

Miss Perfect

When your mother asks you to
clean up your room, do you slap your tail
in defiance?

Do you stomp, spit,
and chew on your sister?

Miss Perfect hopes not.

We must be considerate of our family.

Clean up your room when asked.
Say "I'm sorry" if you slap your tail.

Never stomp or spit.

And ask permission
before chewing on your sister.

Earned the Right

Dear Miss Perfect,

My grandpa wears false teeth.

On Sundays he takes them out and touches
his nose with his tongue.
Sometimes he crosses his eyes at the same time.

My sisters and I laugh.

This makes Grandma angry. She says Grandpa
should keep his teeth in his mouth at all times.
Grandpa says I should write to you.

    Sincerely,
    Susannah Beaver

P.S. I wish I had false teeth.

Dear Miss Beaver,

I assume that your grandfather built dams in his prime,
and that is how he wore out his teeth.

Building dams is hard work. One must fell the trees
by gnawing on them, drag them to the dam,
caulk them with mud, then pat them all down
with one's tail.

It is exhausting. Therefore, I feel your grandfather
has earned the right to take his teeth out to entertain
his grandchildren anytime he pleases.

Happy she has her own beak,

Miss Perfect

P.S. Miss Perfect assumes that Grandpa would
not remove his teeth at the dinner table,
as this would be most inappropriate.

Dear Miss Perfect,

I am playing in my first piano recital this Friday.
My mother wants me to wear a bow tie
on each wrist, but I think bow ties are sissy.

What do you think, Miss Perfect?

 A true artist,
 Alexander Octopus

P.S. I am playing a boogie-woogie.

Dear Mr. Octopus,

I believe you and your mother should compromise.
A bow tie on each wrist might distract you
from playing your best.

A bow tie round the neck, however,
would be most becoming.

What sort of jacket are you wearing? Miss Perfect
believes an electric blue jacket would be very elegant
(if you have not already chosen something else).

Mr. Octopus, you are to be congratulated.
It is not everyone who is invited to play in a recital.

Keeping the beat,

Miss Perfect

A Little Gratitude

Dear Miss Perfect,

Just because I got a lot of presents at my birthday party
doesn't mean I should have to write thank-you notes.

I'm tired. I don't feel like it.
I'd rather stay in bed.

I don't even want to write this letter,
but my mother made me.

What do you think, Miss Perfect?
Do you think I should have to write thank-you notes,
even when I'm tired?

      Needing sleep,
      Wilma Sloth

Dear Miss Sloth,

There are times we must all get out of bed,
Sloths included.

Your friends and family got out of bed
to select and wrap a present.
Now you must thank them by writing
them a note.

It needn't be long:

> *The charm bracelet you gave me*
> *is lovely. I shall treasure*
> *it forever.*

is all you need, along with your salutation and signature.

But Wilma, we must always show our gratitude.

It's only polite,

Miss Perfect

Self-Protection

Dear Miss Perfect,

I just learned that Komodo Dragons
sometimes eat their young.

Miss Perfect, I am a Komodo Dragon.
Do you think my parents will eat me?

Every time Daddy asks for a snack,
I'm afraid he's thinking
of me.

   Anxious fifth-grader,
   Anastasia Komodo

Dear Miss Komodo,

As you have reached the fifth grade,
I think you are large enough that
you do not need to worry.

Just to be safe, however,
I would pour a little extra soap into my bathwater.
Should your daddy take a notion
to swallow you whole, he will immediately
spit you back up.

You might also quiz your parents on
which seasoning they dislike the most.
If they hate pepper, powder yourself with it.

It pays to be cautious,

Miss Perfect

When you are out in the neighborhood,
are you kind to others?

Do you say "I'm sorry"
if you accidentally crush someone?

Are you pleasant to be around?
Quick to extend a pawshake?
Or, if you have no paws,
do you flash a ready smile?

Do you invite the lonely Porcupine to play tag?
Or the shy Hippopotamus to jump rope?

Do you consider the feelings of others?

Dear Miss Perfect,

I am very patriotic.
When I see the flag, I want to salute,
but of course I have no arms to salute with.

My teacher says I should wiggle my tongue.
But I think wiggling my tongue is disrespectful.

What can I do to show my love for my country?

Looking for ideas,
Everett Python

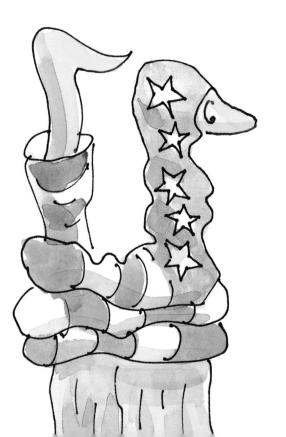

Dear Mr. Python,

Patriotism can be shown in many different ways,
not just with a hand over the heart.

If you can manage it, you might raise your tail
and give it a snappy salute.

Or, on a holiday, roll yourself up
in red, white, and blue.
There's nothing more becoming than
a Python in colors.

Mr. Python, there are many ways
you can show your love for your country.

Just use your imagination,

Miss Perfect

Building for the Future

Dear Miss Perfect,

I love learning new words.
Here are some of my favorites:

> umbrella
> smorgasbord
> perpendicular
> popsicle
> chuckle

Mostly I learn by listening to people. Sometimes I eavesdrop. (Eavesdrop is another favorite word.) Yesterday I heard a policeman talking.

He said some Newts had pulled some "shenanigans" and that the police were in "hot pursuit" and that they had a "rap sheet" out on them.

When I told my mother what I had learned, she said I should never eavesdrop, that it was dishonest and impolite.

What do you think, Miss Perfect?

> Always listening,
> Sylvester Parrot

Dear Mr. Parrot,

The way I see it, words are your business.
In which case, whatever you hear is fair game.

Miss Perfect does not mean to contradict your mother.
She means well, and you should not upset her
by describing in detail where you have picked up
your new words.

Merely file them away. Then look up the definitions.
And then build and build and build your vocabulary.

Mr. Parrot, Miss Perfect has high hopes that someday
you may become a flying dictionary!

In pursuit of knowledge,

Miss Perfect

A Quiet Sit-Down Game

Dear Miss Perfect,

My best friend is a Lion. We used to play
together every day.

But last week I broke his leg.
It was an accident. Honest.

I felt so awful, I cried all night.

Now his mother won't let me play with him anymore.
I ring his doorbell every morning and she
tells me to go away.

What can I do, Miss Perfect?
I miss my friend.

> Feeling lonely,
> Bruno Hippopotamus

Dear Mr. Hippopotamus,

You don't say what you were doing when
you broke your friend's leg. Were you rough-housing?
Did you accidentally sit on him?

Miss Perfect hasn't a clue.
She believes you when you say it was an accident.
She also thinks you must make amends.

How about writing a note of apology?
And then stopping by with a present or two?
Flowers for his mother and a little snack
for your friend of cookies or raw meat.

And then ask your friend's mother if you might stop by
to play a quiet sit-down game such as checkers.
Show her how well mannered you can be.

Let her know that you will never rough-house
in the future and that you can be trusted
not to put your friend in danger.

I am sure you will be successful, as I know
you are truly sorry.

    In the name of peace,

Circle of Friends

Dear Miss Perfect,

We have a family ritual of
checking each other's heads for lice.

Sometimes we sit in a circle.
Mama checks Daddy, Daddy checks
Brother, Brother checks Sister, Sister
checks me, and I check Mama.

I have a friend, Nelda Shrew,
who thinks this is disgusting.
What do you think, Miss Perfect?
Do you think we are disgusting?

    Keeping tidy,
    Miranda Chimp

Dear Miss Chimp,

Keeping one's head free of lice is hardly disgusting. Miss Perfect suspects that Miss Shrew is envious of the care and attention each member of your family gives the others.

Perhaps you could invite her to join your circle. You might say to Miss Shrew, "Nelda, would you care to join us for grooming at six this evening?"

Miss Perfect bets she'll jump at the chance.

Expanding friendship,

Miss Perfect

In Closing

Miss Perfect believes that
a Beast who knows proper behavior
is a happier Beast.

Miss Perfect herself is happy,
living in a small house
at the edge of the North Woods,
where she attempts to do
everything perfectly.

She has a perfect garden,
where she sits at a perfect table,
with a perfect glass of lemonade.
Alas, she has never found the perfect
companion, but she keeps trying.

She hopes that you will
ponder the letters in this book
and their lessons in proper behavior.

And, should you have
any questions of your own, she hopes
you will write to her
at the *Beastly Gazette*.